T0378758

Faces
IN THE
Crowd

CAT JENKINS
KUGU SOYKAN
GINGER TULL

Black Rabbit Tales is an imprint of
Black Rabbit Books
P.O. Box 227
Mankato, MN 56001
www.blackrabbitbooks.com

This library-bound edition is published in 2025 by
Black Rabbit Books, by arrangement with:
Storyshares, LLC
24 N. Bryn Mawr Avenue #340
Bryn Mawr, PA 19010-3304
www.storyshares.org

Printed in China.

Library of Congress Cataloging-in-Publication Data

Names: Jenkins, Cat, author. | Soykan, Kugu, author. | Tull, Ginger, author. Title: Faces in the crowd / Cat Jenkins, Kugu Soykan, Ginger Tull. Description: Mankato, MN: Black Rabbit Books, 2025. | Series: These first letters | Audience: Ages 10–14. | Audience: Grades 4–6. | Summary: "The Think Tank has a winner and Min finds she's not alone in celebrating the power of art, writing, and friendship to make the world a better place"—Provided by publisher. Identifiers: LCCN 2024023316 | ISBN 9781644668993 (library binding) Subjects: LCSH: Readers (Elementary) | English language—Vowels—Juvenile literature. | Comic books, strips, etc.—Authorship—Juvenile fiction. | Comic books, strips, etc.—Competitions—Juvenile fiction. | Children with disabilities—Juvenile fiction. | Self-confidence—Juvenile fiction. | Reading (Elementary) | CYAC: Cartoons and comics—Authorship—Fiction. | Authorship—Fiction. | Contests—Fiction. | People with disabilities—Fiction. | Self-confidence—Fiction. literature. | LCGFT: Readers (Publications). Classification: LCC PE1121 .F584 2025 | DDC 428.6/2—dc23/ eng/20240624 LC record available at https://lccn.loc.gov/2024023170

Aligned with the Science of Reading.
Interest Level: 4th grade and beyond.

Faces in the Crowd

CAT JENKINS
KUGU SOYKAN
GINGER TULL

A Storyshares Decodables Chapter Book

TABLE OF CONTENTS

Met

With a Prize

CAT JENKINS

Met With a Prize

CAT JENKINS

"Met With a Prize"

Magic E: vowel-consonant-e

Magic E

prize	tale	huge	white
time	mine	celebrate	grape
shine	wide	nice	while
rose	tribe	cake	made
complete	beside	take	envelope
fine	came	lake	inside
page	rave	shone	plane
shone	online	jade	mute
line	phone	gave	life
pride	side	chimed	face
came	chose	nine	bite
theme	tune	dine	
mere	made	flutes	

high frequency words

more	took
one	work
where	thought
even	maybe
world	never
find	away
beside	
maybe	

challenge words

graphic	eyes
novel	envelope*
phone	Australia
son	surprise
change	
celebrate	
secrets	
juice	

It was Max's time to shine.

The book that rose out of Min's project was complete.

And it was fine.

Each page shone with the power
of art.

Every line was worthy of pride.

Every story came with a theme
that was more than a mere tale.

"And one of them is mine," said Max.

"The one where even in a world so wide, you can find your tribe."

Soon, their graphic novel would stand beside other works that came from Min's Think Tank.

Max wished he could be there for real to rave, not just online or on a phone.

"Maybe another time," he sighed.

"Son," Max's father said, as he took him to the side. "Your mom and I are filled with pride."

"You chose to change your tune. You made a huge leap and rose up. We would like to celebrate with a prize for your work."

Max thought a prize would be nice.

Maybe Mom would bake a cake.
Maybe they would all take a trip to
a lake.

"What do you think, Biff?" Max asked his cat.

Biff's eyes shone green as jade.

But Biff never gave secrets away.

When the clock chimed nine, it was time to dine.

Max's mom and dad held up flutes of white grape juice.

"To our son," said Max's dad. "As a rule, he can be stubborn as a mule, but he changed his tune and his tone."

"Max, to show our pride, we are giving you a prize," Max's mom said, while tears made her eyes shine.

Then Max's mom gave him an envelope. Inside were plane tickets.

To Australia.

Max was mute with shock.

He would see the graphic novel come to life.

He would see Min face to face.

What could be better?

"Max, Min does not know about this. It will be a surprise for her, too."

And then Max knew what could be better.

His prize was to surprise Min.

SURPRISE

Max had to bite the inside of his lip to keep from crying. All he could say was...

"Thanks."

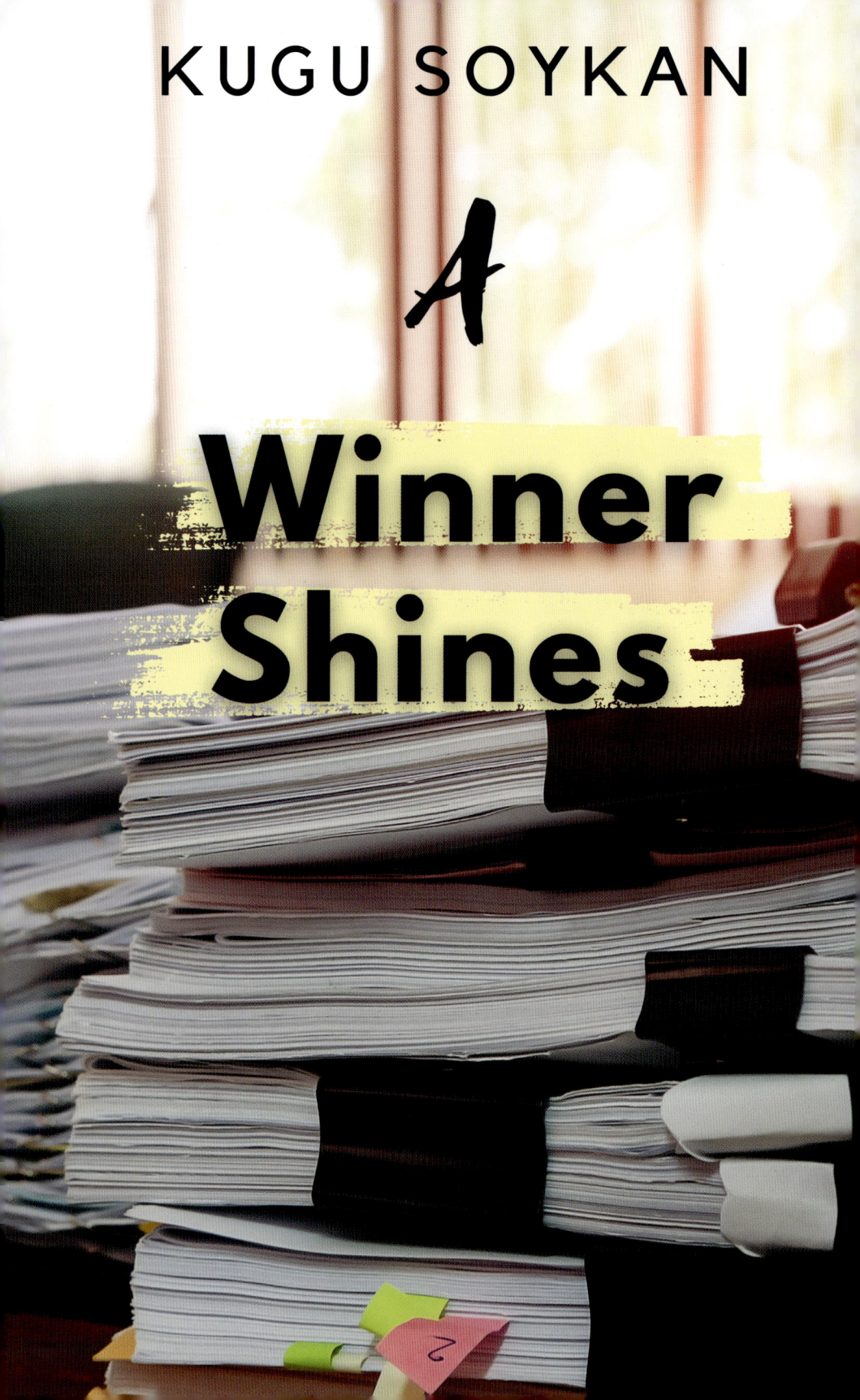

KUGU SOYKAN

A
Winner
Shines

A Winner Shines

KUGU SOYKAN

"A Winner Shines"

Magic E: vowel-consonant-e

Magic E

came	pages	time
Jones	type	cube
cared	share	fine
excited	Wade	hope
wrote	surprised*	
huge	whole	
named	life	
inspired*	waves	
note	make	
grades	chose	
envelope*	complete	

high frequency words

ready	about
loved	across
student	world
some	over
someone	other
teachers	many
school	
remembered	

challenge words

program	envelope*	surprised*
voices	impressed	London
submitted	Benin	England
inspired*	Ecuador	Australia
entry	North Carolina	
celebration	science	

*These challenge words also use the focus sound.

"Are you ready to check out what came out of the Think Tank contest?" asked Ms. Jones.

Ms. Jones led the Think Tank program. Ms. Jones cared about the Think Tank program so much. She loved to hear student voices.

Today, she would view the entries for the contest with some other teachers from Min's school.

They were all very excited to read what the students wrote.
There was a huge stack waiting for them.

The first one they read was Min's.

"This is odd. This is a graphic novel and has been submitted by someone named Max," said Ms. Jones. "But we should still read it. If a friend is so inspired to submit an idea, it must be very good."

The other works were not graphic novels. This helped Min's to stand out.

The teachers really liked the drawings and colors. It made them feel happy to be there, reading her entry.

They took note of this.

Ms. Ling was the art teacher for all grades at Min's school. She was very excited to see the Golden Week celebration in the graphic novel.

Ms. Ling remembered going to Golden Week every year with her family. She remembered singing and getting red envelope bills. It was always such a huge celebration.

The teachers were very impressed by how many friends Min did her project with.

Her graphic novel had points of view and cultures from Benin to Ecuador to North Carolina!

As Ms. Jones and the rest of the teachers kept flipping the pages, they saw more and more. This was just the type of entry they were looking for.

Then they saw the pages about Carlos and his Pic-Share page.

Mr. Wade, the grade 8 science teacher at Min's school, was very surprised.

He had wanted to go to Ecuador for his whole life.

Now, he was reading about it.

On weekends, Mr. Wade helped out on the coast.

He helped clean the beach near the Great Barrier Reef. He loved to see the waves.

Mr. Wade connected with the pages.

They lived across the world, but the problems that kept Mr. Wade up at night seemed to keep the students in the book up at night, too.

Ms. Jones was so inspired by Arin and Rakesh's stories.

Ms. Jones was from London, England.

When she was ten, her mom chose to move them to Australia.

It was hard for her to make new friends, but with time, Australia became her home. She knew about some of the challenges Arin and Rakesh wrote about.

Ms. Jones took note of this, too.

They flipped to the last page and the graphic novel was complete!

Ms. Jones and the rest of the teachers were so sad it was over.

"We will have to look at that again some time!" said Ms. Lin.

Next, it was time for them to read the other works students had submitted.

There were so many that they made a cube on the desk.

A lot of them were great. Others were fine.

Some students at Min's school wrote about hardships.

Others wrote about ways to fix life's problems.

But there was only one entry that stuck in their minds: Min's.

"I think it is clear who the winner is," said Mr. Wade.

"We agree with you," said the other teachers.

They were all thinking of Min's entry. Her entry gave them hope.

Later that day, Ms. Jones wrote to Max.

New Message

To maxlovesbball@biff.me

Subject A Think Tank Winner!

Dear Max,

I am so happy to tell you that we chose Min's entry as the grand winner for the Think Tank contest.

I wanted to tell you first, just in case you want to surprise her. You and your friends' stories inspired all of the judges.

We are very happy to get to hear your ideas for making student voices heard.

Best wishes,

Ms. Jones

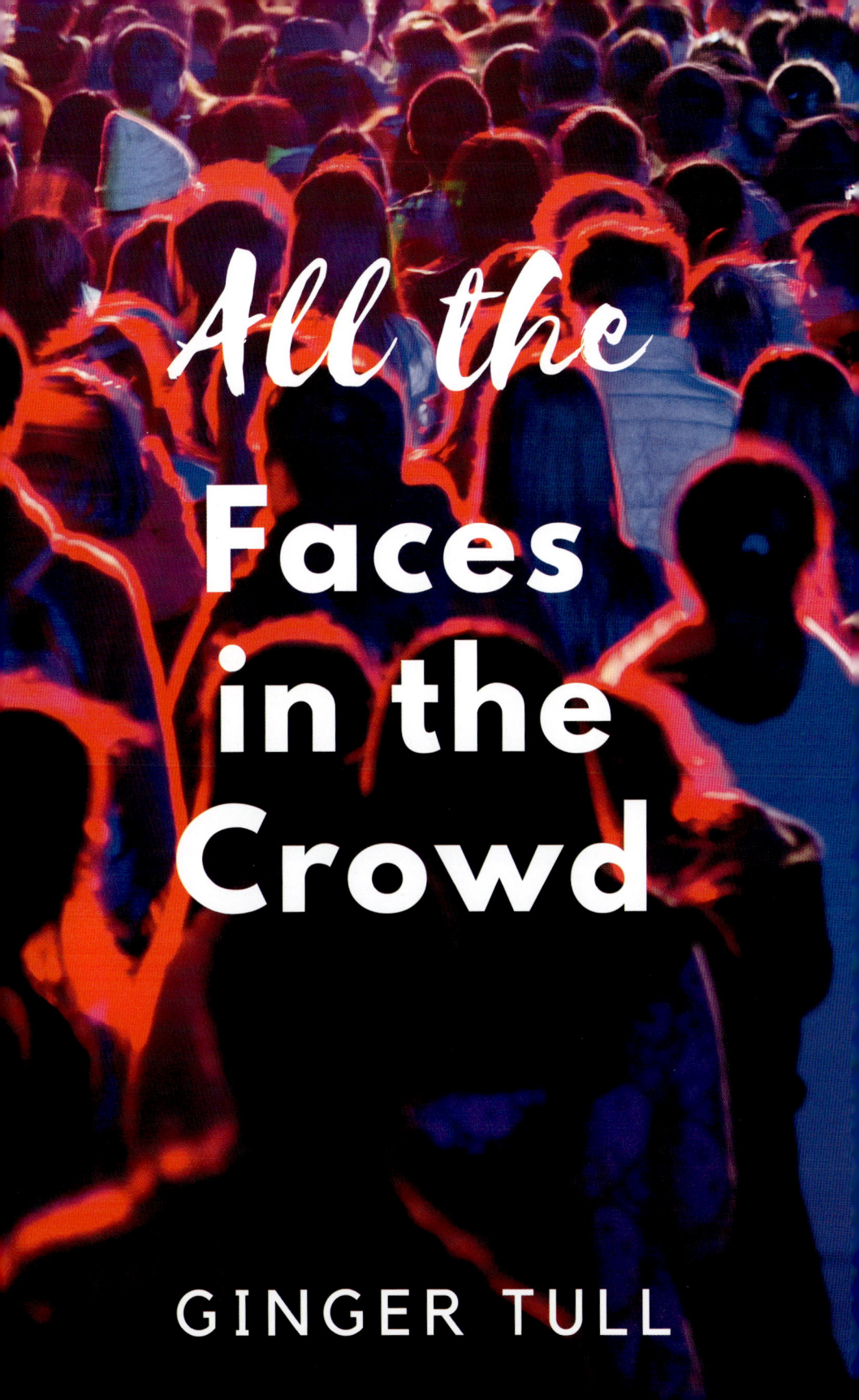

All the

Faces in the Crowd

GINGER TULL

All the Faces in the Crowd

GINGER TULL

"All the Faces in the Crowd"

Magic E: vowel-consonant-e

Magic E

home	mute	changed	glide	pride
drove	spoke	side	gave	make
while	scared	close	wave	take
rode	stage	shone	rose	score
share	alone	daze	spoke	true
wore	excited	place	dive	
fine	whole	gaze	chose	
made	rude	male	here	
brave	shame	confused	smile	
face	dude	joke	rules	
code	globe	cake	envelope*	
glare	line	close	blazed	

high frequency words

today	looked
again	somehow
number	coming
people	again
there	talked
don't	tried
know	goodbye
knew	lose

challenge words

uneasy	American
culture	Seattle
humble	Australia
won	heart
group	distance
laughed	surprise*
event	published
wheelchair	

Ba and Min left home for the Great Hall. Ba drove while Min rode in the car.

Today the Think Tank would share Min's name as winner of the contest!

Min wore a fine dress and made a brave face.

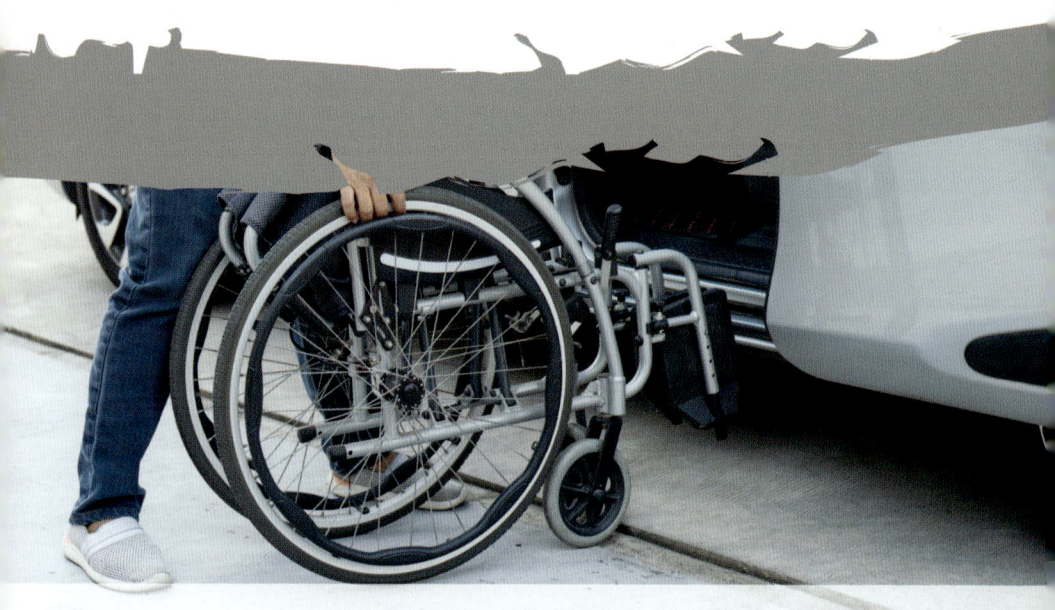

"Min?" Ba asked.

Min was mute.

"Min? Min, are you okay?" Ba asked again.

"Sorry, Ba," Min spoke.

Min was scared to go on stage alone.

"Min, a great number of people will be there. Are you scared?" Ba asked.

Min said, "I feel excited and scared, Ba."

Min felt uneasy about the win. She didn't do the work alone. Min's culture was to be humble. She wanted to thank the people from the Think Tank. But it was the whole team that won. Min did not want to be rude.

"I want to share the prize with my group," Min said.

"It is a shame they can't be here to share it. What will you say when they say you are the winner?" Ba asked.

"Dude, I don't know," Min said with a grin.

Ba laughed! He could see that Min had changed. She had shown growth and self-esteem.

"Dude, you got this!" Ba teased. They both laughed.

At the event, Ba and Min sat on the side. Min wanted to be close to the ramp. The stage looked so big. Min was planning how to get her wheelchair on the stage.

People filled the Great Hall. Bright lights shone on the stage. Min was in a daze. During the program, Min looked around the whole place. There were so many people!

Min's gaze fell on a face she knew. This male looked like Max. Min was confused because Max was American. He lived in Seattle, not Australia.

This was not a joke. Somehow Max was there! Then she saw someone glide up next to Max.

Was that... Whit? And Destiny? There were Arin and Rakesh! And Sara. Someone gave a wave. It was... Max!

Min's heart swelled with joy! She wanted to go to them, but the person on stage rose and spoke. It was time to dive in.

"Hello, and thank you for coming," the host said.

Min chose to look back at her friends again. She loved that they were there! Her face was bright with a smile.

The host talked more. She shared about the Think Tank contest rules and code. Then it was time for Min to go on stage.

"Min is this year's winner of the Think Tank competition!" the host said.

She was telling Min to join her on stage. Min spun her wheels fast and rode up the ramp. The glare from the lights got in her eyes on the stage. Min tried to see her friends. She smiled at her crew as she was handed the award. The crowd clapped for quite a long time.

Then, Min spoke. "Thank you. But I share this award with my whole team. They came from around the globe. I want to ask my friends to join me on stage!"

A line of Min's friends began to file onto the stage. The crowd cheered like before. Ba was more happy for Min than she had ever seen him.

To celebrate, the friends went to get a cake. Min was truly surprised that they were there. They hugged and shared stories.

Soon, they had to say goodbye. The distance would not keep them from being close friends. Max had one more surprise for Min. Max gave her a red rose and a red envelope.

Min smiled and her face blazed red. She opened the red envelope from Max.

"Yay! The *Letters to Transform the World* book will be published!"

Min was shocked! Her eyes were wide with pride.

"This is SO COOL! How did you make this happen?" she asked Max.

Max said, "The comic was so good, it had to be published. If basketball has taught me anything..."

The friends rose up excitedly around Max and Min. Before Max could say it, they all yelled, "You lose all the shots you fail to take!"

"Score!" Max yelled, and the whole crew laughed. Their joy filled the room. The group of friends held hands and smiled with true joy.

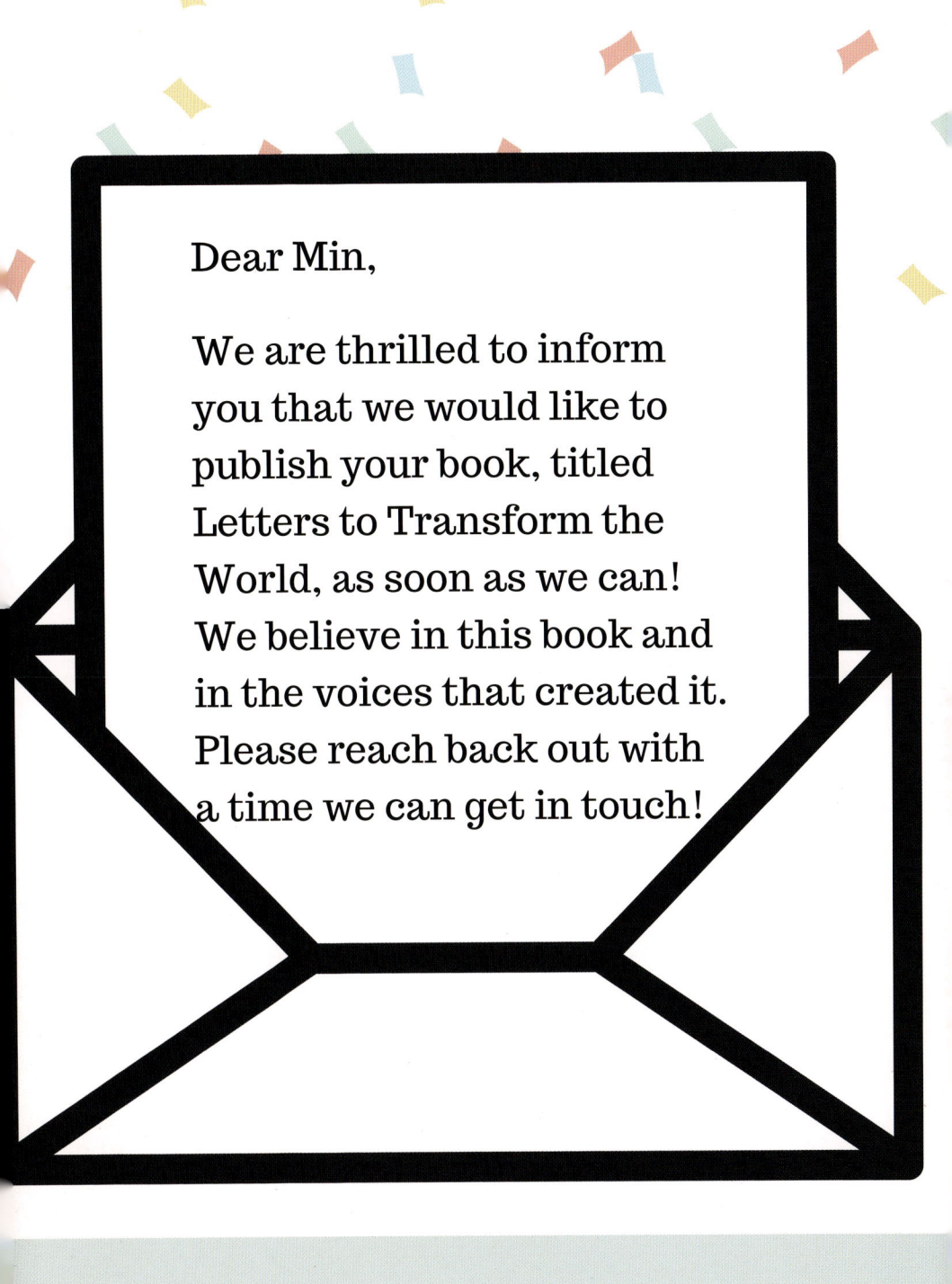

Dear Min,

We are thrilled to inform
you that we would like to
publish your book, titled
Letters to Transform the
World, as soon as we can!
We believe in this book and
in the voices that created it.
Please reach back out with
a time we can get in touch!

Letters Transform the World

KUGU SOYKAN

Letters Transform the World

KUGU SOYKAN

"Letters Transform the World"

Magic E: vowel-consonant-e

Magic E

value	homesick
globe	continue*
online	make
home	excited
share	notes
page	
whale	
write	
analyze*	
whole	
time	

high frequency words

used	love
only	live
friend	able
learned	neighborhood
writing	
have	
school	
sometimes	

challenge words

taught	oxygen
found	analyze*
cooking	magazine
videos	important
passionate	endangered
Bahamas	species
concerned	ecosystem
dolphins	culture
continue	beautiful

I used to only think about playing basketball with my team, the Mets.

Until I joined the LEX program and met my friend, Min.

I learned the value of reading and writing. Now, I have my own art club at school!

Min taught me that sometimes, art can express what words cannot.

We put out a call across the globe, asking students everywhere: What is important to you?

My name is Sara. I live with my Aunt Mal.

I used to have low self-esteem before I found what I love to do... cooking!

Sometimes, I film videos about the farm I live on.

Here is the winning dish: fried chicken!

After hosting a cook-off to raise funds to clean up beaches, I had much more self-esteem!

BEFORE:

AFTER:

I'm Destiny! I'm passionate about self-esteem and beach clean-ups!

My online show, TeenTalk, is all about self-esteem, something that is very important to me.

TeenTalk

Once I saw all of the trash on the beaches in my home, the Bahamas, I planned a beach clean-up.

I was so concerned, because trash is a peril to marine life.

I'm Whit. I live in Benin and I love to go whale watching.

This is my ship, the Write Wing.

This is the book I use to take notes and record my findings.

While going whale watching, I started a study on West African manatees.

This is a West African manatee.

I gather data and analyze it. I will submit this study to the Teen Jazz magazine.

It is so important to help endangered species. They affect the whole ecosystem!

I'm Arin. I moved to the United States this year.

And I am Rakesh. I moved to a new neighborhood.

We have been friends for a very long time.

Sometimes it is very hard to adapt to a new culture.

Both Arin and Rakesh are feeling homesick for their friendship.

But, with the internet, we found a way to continue our friendship!

With the power of reading and writing, each and every one of us was able to connect with people that make change around the world. We are excited to leave our mark on this beautiful planet.

About the Authors

Cat Jenkins lives in the Pacific Northwest where the weather is often conducive to long hours before a keyboard. Her stories in humor, fantasy, speculative fiction, and horror have been published both online and in print. Her first novel, *Sara When She Chooses,* was published by Bedazzled Ink Publishing in May 2018. Cat's blog can be found at: catjenkinsdotcom.wordpress.com.

Kugu Soykan enjoys writing about critical global issues, supporting children's rights, volunteering, and taking part in civil services projects. Her two Storyshares books received honorable mention awards in the 2021 and 2022 Storyshares Story of the Year Contests. She is a Congressional Award Gold Medal and STEM STAR recipient. She is the winner of the 2022 European Union Year of the Youth Writing Contest, judged by the European Parliament members, and has taken part in volunteering projects such as Ukrainian War Refugees Camp in Belgium, EU Youth Development Program in Germany, European Communities Ethnic, Cultural, and Religious program in Israel. She is a member of the European Union Youth Forum and UNICEF USA Advocate, where she acts as the voice for young people and strives for societies where young people are empowered and encouraged to achieve their fullest potential as global citizens.

Ginger Tull is a a writer from the hot, dusty, dry Four Corners area of New Mexico. She is a film actor, screenplay writer, and aspiring fiction author. Ginger is a terrible cook but a decent baker. Except for snakes, she enjoys the liveliness of the outdoors and spends way too much time hiking, mountain biking and skiing with her family. She also tends to nine boisterous chickens, three colorful bee hives and keeps her 100-pound dog, Renzo The Magnificent, happy by taking him on long hikes through the sagebrush and sand near her desert home.